For my two wee stars, Alice and Archie – S.H.

For Sophie and Alex – S.M.

Star in the Jar

SAM HAY

SARAH MASSINI

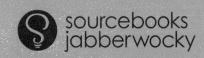

sourcebooks
jabberwocky

My little brother likes looking for treasure.

Tickly treasure...

Glittery treasure...

even trash-can treasure!

But one day he found
something extra special.

So special I thought it
must belong to someone else.

We asked the helpful girl from school.
But she said it wasn't hers.

We showed it to the lunch lady.
But it wasn't hers, either.

We asked the sheriff.
But he shook his head.

The fairies hadn't lost it.

Nor had the wizards.

"If no one has lost it,"
my little brother said,
"that means I can keep it!"

My little brother
loved his new treasure.

He put it in a jar and
carried it everywhere.

As the day turned into night, the little treasure got shinier.
But it didn't look happy.

Then my little brother spotted something.
Up high, in the dark, dark, sky, there was a message!

"It's here!" my little brother shouted to the sky.
But the little star's friends were too far away to hear.

We had to help the star get back home.

We tried climbing up high,

teaching it to fly,

and bouncing the star back up to the sky.

But nothing worked.
Maybe the little star would have
to stay in the jar forever.

Then an idea popped into my head.
I raced inside and looked in every
cabinet and every drawer.

I found flashlights and twinkling lights.

Book lamps and bike lights.

Glow sticks and head lamps.

And we sent
a message back...

Then the sky began to crackle.

And fizz.

And the stars joined together and made
a long swirly, whirly, sparkly silver chain.
All the way down to our backyard...

And they lifted their
little friend gently
back up to the sky.

My little brother felt sad.
He'd lost his special treasure.

But then...

Thank yOu
Friend

He realized he hadn't lost his treasure.

He'd made a friend.

A forever friend who would
twinkle him to sleep, every night.

Goodnight, Star.

Published by Sourcebooks Jabberwocky, an imprint of Sourcebooks, Inc.

P.O. Box 4410, Naperville, Illinois 60567-4410

(630) 961-3900

Fax: (630) 961-2168

sourcebooks.com

Originally published in 2018 in Great Britain by Egmont UK Limited.

Library of Congress Cataloging-in-Publication Data is on file with the publisher.

Source of Production: Tien Wah Press, Malaysia

Date of Production: April 2018

Run Number: 5012049

Printed and bound in Malaysia.

10 9 8 7 6 5 4 3 2 1